BEGINNINGS

Aurora
Plays the Part

BY TESSA ROEHL

ILLUSTRATED BY
THE DISNEY STORYBOOK ART TEAM

Random House 🏠 New York

For Bonnie
—T. R.

Copyright © 2018 Disney Enterprises, Inc. All rights reserved. Published in
the United States by Random House Children's Books, a division of Penguin
Random House LLC, 1745 Broadway, New York, NY 10019, and in Canada by
Penguin Random House Canada Limited, Toronto, in conjunction with Disney
Enterprises, Inc. Random House and the colophon are registered trademarks of
Penguin Random House LLC.

rhcbooks.com

ISBN 978-0-7364-3795-0 (trade) — ISBN 978-0-7364-8260-8 (lib. bdg.)

Printed in the United States of America

10 9 8 7 6 5 4 3

Book design by Jenna Huerta & Betty Avila

This book has been officially leveled by using the F&P Text Level Gradient™
Leveling System.

Random House Children's Books supports the First Amendment and celebrates
the right to read.

Chapter 1
Briar Rose

Briar Rose dreamed a lot. She dreamed at night, and she dreamed during the day. Most of the time, Rose was content with her simple life in the forest. Her aunts had set boundaries for how far she was allowed to wander beyond their modest cottage. As Rose grew, the area within these borders sometimes felt lonely and small, but her dreams opened her world much wider.

Rose dreamed of following the forest animals when they scampered away after visiting her. She dreamed of setting foot in a place beyond her boundaries. She dreamed of meeting someone new. Someone her age. Someone she could talk to.

It wasn't as though Rose didn't know anything about the world beyond the forest. She'd heard about other kingdoms, lands, and villages in the stories her aunts had told her. But Rose was growing frustrated that she couldn't see more of this world with her own eyes. Her aunts had a reason for being so strict, of course. Their greatest job and biggest worry was protecting Princess

Aurora. They'd even re-named her Briar Rose for her safety. But Rose didn't know her true identity.

Her aunts defended their rules, saying the world outside the boundaries "wasn't safe *yet.*" Rose clung to the word "yet." It meant that someday her world would open. She just didn't know when.

Every day, Rose would walk to one of the four borders: the blackberry bushes to the north (with the juiciest berries to pick), the stream to the east (her favorite place to sing with the birds), the cliffs to the south (with the most wonderful view of the valley), and the great fallen oak tree to the west (the perfect place to search for fairies, which she'd yet to find). Recently, Rose had started asking her aunts if she could go a little farther—just a few steps beyond the borders.

First, Rose would ask her aunt Flora, the eldest and sternest of the three aunts. Aunt Flora would always respond with a firm "No."

Next, Rose would go to her aunt Fauna. Gentle and petite, Aunt Fauna would also say, "No," but would follow it with a "dear."

And then there was Aunt Merryweather, who would frown sympathetically and say, "Not today, Rose."

Whenever Rose left the cottage, they would call, *"Don't speak to strangers!"* That seemed silly to Rose. *What strangers?* Other than the milkmaid, the miller, and the occasional village delivery boy, Rose had never met another person in the forest.

One day, after putting on her shawl and grabbing her basket, Rose headed toward the east boundary, where the stream flowed past the blackberry bushes. She picked berries, humming a tune while the birds harmonized with her melody. Her mind wandered: she imagined her shawl was her costume, the birds were her chorus, and the babbling brook was a roar of applause from a watching crowd.

But something caught Rose's eye. She saw a white streak. Then she heard a *splash!* The birds fluttered off their branches as a mother rabbit and her children hopped across a log to the opposite bank. One bunny was struggling in the shallow water. The bunny's family hadn't noticed he'd fallen! The water rushed around the young rabbit's neck as he tried to pull himself to the bank.

Rose dropped her basket and ran to the stream. She plunged her hands into the cold water and felt for a slimy branch that had caught the rabbit's paw. Rose pulled the branch away and scooped the wet bunny into her arms. She wrapped the shivering

creature in her shawl and leapt out of the stream. The rabbits were getting farther and farther away. Rose chased after them, calling out.

As she neared the rabbit family, the mother turned—and her ears immediately drooped against her head. Rose caught up and lowered the bunny gently to the grass. His mother nuzzled him, and his siblings gathered around, snuggling him with warmth. The mother rabbit rubbed Rose's hand in thanks.

Rose patted her head. "Well, that was scary. I'm glad he's all right."

The mother rabbit wiggled her nose

and hopped away, her children close behind her. The family disappeared into a hole in the side of the hill. When the pounding in Rose's chest quieted, she realized that she could no longer hear the familiar rush of the stream.

Rose was in an open field. She'd never been here before. She'd never *seen* this place before. She must have traveled beyond her aunts' borders—for the first time in her life. She swiveled around and, to her relief, spied the stream and the forest in the distance.

Rose took another look at the field. She wished she could explore this new place. Were there animals here she hadn't met? What lay beyond the hilltop? Could there be other people nearby?

But she had already strayed too far.

Rose had just started toward the forest when she saw it: a small briar patch was growing at the base of the hill, and among the brambles were vibrant pink roses. *Briar Rose,* she thought. *That's my name.*

Rose's hands were inches away from a flower when a noise startled her. *CRACK!* Twigs snapped. She craned her neck to see what kind of animal might be headed her way.

Then Rose stared, for she couldn't believe her eyes. Walking toward her was no animal. It was a girl.

Chapter 2
The Stranger

"Hello! Hello over there!" The girl had spotted Rose, too.

Of course she did, Rose thought, feeling foolish. *I'm not invisible!*

"Hello," Rose called to the girl, who had almost reached her. *What am I doing?* Rose wondered. First she'd broken the rule of leaving the forest borders, and now she was speaking to a real, live stranger!

"Oh!" the girl said, noticing the roses in the briar patch. Her long blond hair, similar to Rose's, fell forward as she leaned to smell the petals. "What beautiful flowers! I've got to take one back to my grandmother."

Rose's aunts' warnings about strangers rang in her ears. She took a few steps back toward the forest.

The girl noticed Rose's hesitation. "I'm sorry. I didn't introduce myself. I'm Grace. My grandmother sent me to find water. Our acting troupe's caravan has broken down by the road." Grace motioned behind her.

The road? Rose wondered. She'd had no idea there was a road nearby. "I can show you to a stream," she offered. She hated to leave anyone thirsty.

"Wonderful!" Grace exclaimed, and Rose led her to the stream.

Grace kneeled over the running water, dipping in one of several canteens she'd brought with her. Rose watched. She wanted to stay. She wanted to ask the girl question after question about what her acting troupe was like, who she knew, and where she'd come from. But her aunts had forbidden her to speak to strangers. This whole afternoon had been forbidden!

So by the time Grace looked up and asked her name, Rose had already slipped into the trees and headed for home.

Rose's home was the same humble cottage she'd always known, with its thatched roof, its chimney puffing smoke, and its small window upstairs by the bed where she slept. But

Rose did not feel the same. She'd been to a new place. She'd met a new person.

Rose walked inside to find Aunt Fauna sitting on a chair, mending a torn pillowcase. Aunt Flora and Aunt Merryweather were at the hearth, bickering over dinner.

"I'm home!" Rose called as she hung up her shawl. Aunt Flora came forward to greet her, leaving Aunt Merryweather to sneak an extra dash of spice into the boiling stew.

"Why, Rose," Aunt Flora said, noticing Rose's empty hands, "where's your basket?"

Rose realized that in the commotion of the bunny rescue and meeting Grace, she'd forgotten to retrieve her basket. "Oh, dear.

I dropped it in the forest," she said. "But I'll tell you why."

Aunt Merryweather and Aunt Flora came closer to Aunt Fauna, who was sewing at the table. Rose told her aunts about her day, from picking berries to saving the bunny to showing Grace the stream.

Her aunts listened with worried but calm expressions. Rose hoped they wouldn't be cross with her for breaking the rules.

Aunt Flora began. "Rose, thank you for telling us what happened. I understand why you felt the need to cross the boundaries."

"We're proud of you for rescuing the bunny, dear," Aunt Fauna said.

"But you must never leave the forest again," Aunt Flora said. "We set those boundaries for a reason—to make sure you stay where we know you are safe. If there's an emergency, you come find us and we'll take care of it."

"But what if there isn't time? The bunny could have drowned," Rose protested.

"We may be a bit older, but we can move faster than you think," Aunt Merryweather replied.

"Well, what about Grace? It sounds like she and her family, or troupe"—Rose wasn't really sure what a troupe was—"may be in trouble. Should we go help them?"

Aunt Flora frowned. She turned to Aunt Fauna and Aunt Merryweather. "We don't want them spending too much time exploring around here," she said.

Aunt Fauna shook her head. "Or drawing too much attention."

"If we help them, they might move along faster," Aunt Merryweather suggested.

"Or is it better to stay away, hidden in the cottage, until they leave?" Aunt Fauna asked.

Aunt Flora placed her chin in her hands. "I'm just not sure."

They were discussing this as though

Rose weren't standing right there. She couldn't believe what she was hearing. *Stay away? Hide?* "Of course we *must* help!"

Rose's aunts looked at her in surprise.

She continued, "We know this forest better than anyone. These people didn't even know where to find water! How can we stay hidden when help is needed?"

"Now, Rose," Aunt Flora said. "How many times must we tell you? It's not safe out there."

"I know, but—" Rose began.

"Our job is to protect *you,* Rose. Not anyone else," Aunt Fauna said.

Aunt Merryweather nodded. "Helping others is important, but not if it interferes with protecting you and this cottage."

Upset, Rose ran to her bedroom. She didn't want to hear any more. Not helping just didn't feel right.

Chapter 3
Beyond the Borders

Rose stayed in bed all night without going down for supper. She thought about what Grace and her troupe might be like and what kind of trouble they might be in. She pictured a rowdy group of adventurers, people who'd seen the world. She imagined some awful force keeping them from their journey—a terrible dragon in a distant cave or goblins up to no good. She thought about this until she fell asleep.

When she awoke the next day, she was hungry from skipping dinner. She went downstairs, hoping her aunts weren't angry with her for having raised her voice the night before.

As soon as she entered the kitchen, Aunt Flora whisked her to the table. Then she set some eggs and slices of fresh-baked bread before her. Rose was grateful that the bread had been made by Aunt Flora and therefore was warm and tasty and looked the way bread ought to look. When Aunt

Merryweather or Aunt Fauna was in charge of the baking, things often didn't turn out quite right.

Before Rose could take a bite, her aunts gathered in front of her. Rose gulped, hoping she wasn't about to receive another lecture. But Aunt Fauna spoke in her usual sweet voice. "Rose, Flora and I will set out today to find the troupe and see if they could use any help."

Gratitude washed over Rose.

"We are glad we've raised such a kind, strong girl," Aunt Flora said. "Your eagerness to help others is a lovely quality."

"Can I come along?" Rose asked.

Aunt Flora shook her head. "No. Absolutely not."

Rose slumped in her chair. She wished she had more of a voice in what she was and wasn't allowed to do.

"There, there, Rose," Aunt Fauna soothed, patting Rose's shoulder. "I'll tell you all about it when I return."

Aunt Fauna put on her traveling cloak, Aunt Flora heaved a covered basket from the counter, and the two left the cottage. Rose finished her breakfast quietly while Aunt Merryweather fumbled over putting away the eggs and bread. As her aunt made a mess of rearranging the shelves, Rose took the chance to grab her shawl and slip out the front door.

It didn't take Rose long to catch up to Aunt Flora and Aunt Fauna—she had mastered all the shortcuts in the forest. Her aunts were almost to the stream when Rose stepped onto the path in front of them.

"Rose!" Aunt Fauna said in surprise.

"Please," Rose begged, "let me come along."

Aunt Flora's face was stern. "We told you very clearly. You are not allowed to leave the forest."

"I know, but . . ." A tear sprang to Rose's eye. She couldn't bear it anymore. She felt trapped while the whole world spun around her, just out of reach.

Aunt Fauna wiped away the tear spilling

down Rose's cheek. "There, there, child," she said as Rose sniffled.

Aunt Flora sighed. "Hand Fauna your shawl and put on her cloak," she said.

Aunt Fauna held her traveling cloak out to Rose, and Rose did as her aunt had asked. Aunt Fauna draped Rose's shawl around her own shoulders and lifted the cloak's hood onto Rose's head so it shadowed her face. "Keep the hood like this, all right?"

Rose nodded eagerly, causing the hood to slip back from her head. She quickly put it back on.

"Just this once," Aunt Flora said.

Rose followed her aunts, her heart leaping with excitement when they crossed the stream, her *old* boundary. Since her aunts traveled to nearby villages from time to time to get food and supplies, Rose assumed they knew just where this mysterious road was.

After a long walk, they crested a hill just as the sun rose in the sky. Rose saw what could only be Grace's troupe below, spread out next to a winding dirt path: the road.

Rose and her aunts descended the hillside toward the troupe's campsite. Several wagons were parked near the road, forming a semicircle, and tents were pitched around

the meadow. In the middle of the wagon circle was a large, blazing fire. People were gathered in small groups, talking and laughing. A large crowd was assembled around the fire, playing instruments and dancing. Rose had never seen such a merry sight.

"Let's find the person in charge," Aunt Flora said.

They wandered into the camp. No one seemed startled by the newcomers, and several people even raised their cups in cheers and welcome.

Within moments, a tall man with a curly mustache and a top hat approached them. He grinned down at Aunt Flora, Aunt Fauna, and Rose. He was almost twice their height. "Well, hello! Welcome to the temporary home of the Errant Band of Actors." The man gave a slight bow. "My name is Alexandre Wellington. I'm the director of this talented troupe."

"We heard you might be in need of help, sir," Aunt Flora said.

Alexandre held a hand to his heart. "Ah, yes. One of the perils of being on the road. Not one of us woke the other night to hear the bandits robbing our wagons. They took everything they could find, from food to water to our wagon wheels!"

Rose saw that, indeed, one of the wagons was sitting straight on the ground, no wheels in sight!

"Luckily," Alexandre said with a wink, "they left our costumes. Fools! The costumes are the most valuable items. In our hearts, anyway."

Rose felt a tap on her shoulder. It was Grace, wrapped in a red cape.

"You're here!" Grace greeted Rose. Rose glanced nervously at her aunts. They were distracted, handing Alexandre the food basket and inspecting the wagons.

"How did you recognize me?" Rose asked, checking to make sure her hood was still in place.

Grace raised her eyebrows. "Do you see any other kids here?" Rose looked around and realized it was true: there were no other children in the camp.

"Do you like my cape?" Grace held the pretty red material out for Rose to take a closer look.

"I love it," Rose replied.

Grace tugged on her sleeve. "You have to

come and meet my grandmother!" she said.

"Where is she?" Rose asked. Grace pointed to a nearby tent. Rose stole another glance at her aunts, who were still talking with Alexandre. *I won't be wandering far,* Rose told herself. She wanted to see more. Who knew when she would get this chance again? She followed Grace to the tent.

Chapter 4
Madam Talia

Inside Grace's grandmother's tent were costumes, wigs, and props galore. Along one wall were fine gowns in every color imaginable. Along another wall were modest village clothes. Then there were grand animal costumes, masks, silly shoes, funny hats, and an open trunk overflowing with jewelry, crowns, and armor.

A woman emerged from the back of the tent. "This is my grandmother," Grace said. Grace's grandmother's face was marked with dark, sharp scars that looked painful. Rose hoped she wasn't being rude by staring.

"Call me Madam Talia. You must be the girl who showed our Grace the water yesterday," the woman said.

Rose knew she shouldn't give her name to a stranger, but as she gazed into Madam Talia's face, she had a sense that the woman could be trusted. "I'm Rose," she said, and gave a small curtsy.

"Grandma makes all our costumes,"

Grace said as she swooped her cape around dramatically.

Madam Talia laughed. "I couldn't ask for a better job," she said, ruffling Grace's hair.

"So your troupe puts on plays? Where?" Rose asked. She was fascinated.

"Everywhere." Madam Talia shrugged. "We travel from village to village. Most of our group are actors, some are responsible for props or sets, and I make the costumes."

"And my dad, Alexandre, is the director," Grace added.

"I would love to perform on a stage," Rose said. She spotted something large behind Madam Talia. "Ohh," she breathed. "May I look at it?" She pointed to the object.

Madam Talia nodded. "This is a costume piece I'm working on for the villain in our latest play. Her name is Maleficent."

It was a large black headdress with what looked like horns coming out of either side. Rose was enchanted and terrified at the same time. She was just reaching to touch a horn when she heard Aunt Flora call out behind her.

"Rose!"

Rose turned around. Her aunt's face was ghostly white. "Don't touch that!" she cried, her voice full of fear.

Rose snatched her hand to her chest, suddenly frightened.

"You needn't worry; it's only a costume," Madam Talia said to Aunt Flora.

Aunt Flora hurried over to Rose and clutched the hand that had almost touched the horn. "Costume or not, how could you keep a symbol of such evil?" Aunt Flora asked Madam Talia.

Rose gulped and looked at the headdress. Symbol of *evil*?

"Maleficent has done great harm to many. We tell her stories so we don't forget that others are still subject to her cruelty," Madam Talia said calmly.

Aunt Flora shook her head, lips pursed. She pulled Rose toward the door gently but firmly. "Such a thing has no place near children. You ought to get rid of it!"

Aunt Fauna stood outside the tent with Alexandre and two other men. "Is everything all right?" she asked Aunt Flora.

"I'm afraid not," Aunt Flora said. "There's a model of Maleficent's horns inside the tent."

Aunt Fauna's hands fluttered to her mouth in surprise.

"It's only a costume," Rose said. "Why are you so upset?"

Aunt Flora kneeled before Rose, speaking softly. "That costume represents a terrible fairy. There is evil in the world, Rose. Do you understand?"

Rose thought about the bandits who had stranded the troupe. "Yes, I do," she answered. "But Madam Talia is not evil. She only made a costume."

Aunt Flora smiled a sad smile. "I'm sure she's not evil or even bad at all, Rose. Most people are not. Most people are good and

true, worth knowing and worth helping."
Her aunt adjusted the hood around Rose's
head. "But evil can be disguised, sweet child.
It can hide in the places you least expect.
When you're older, you will understand."

Before Rose could protest, Grace came
out of the tent. "My grandmother doesn't
mean any harm," she said to Aunt Flora and
Aunt Fauna. "I promise."

"You must be the girl Rose told us about,"
Aunt Flora said.

"I'm Grace," Grace replied with a polite
smile.

"I'm sorry, Grace," Aunt Flora said.
"What that fairy has done—" She shook her

head instead of finishing her sentence.

What do my aunts know about fairies?
Rose wondered. *What do they know about
Maleficent?*

Aunt Fauna spoke next. "Rose, we've
decided to go with Alexandre and the others
to help them find the parts they need to
repair their wagons. We'll escort you back to
the cottage and leave straight from there."

"Could I come along?" Grace asked.
"I should get more water anyway."

"Is it all right with your father?" Aunt
Flora eyed Alexandre.

"Of course," Alexandre said.

* * *

On the walk back to the forest, Rose and Grace stayed a few paces behind Aunt Flora, Aunt Fauna, and the others. The girls talked so much, it soon seemed they'd known each other forever.

Grace spoke of all the villages and kingdoms she'd seen, and the fascinating and important people she'd met. She also talked about her favorite village, one where she had hoped her family could one day stay for good.

Rose shared tales of all the animals she'd made friends with in the forest, including the rabbit family that had led her to Grace the day before. She spoke quietly about how her aunts tried so hard to keep her safe, and how she wished she could be a little *less* safe if it meant seeing new things and meeting new people.

Soon the group reached the stream. They were back inside Rose's boundaries. "Aunt Flora, Aunt Fauna—do you mind if I keep Grace company while she collects her water?" Rose didn't want her time with Grace to end just yet.

"You'll head to the cottage straight after?" Aunt Flora asked.

Rose nodded.

"Then we'll say our goodbyes now," Aunt Flora said, wrapping Rose in a hug. "The journey will take three days. We'll tell Merryweather the plan, gather supplies, and be on our way."

Aunt Fauna hugged Rose next. "Take care, Briar Rose."

"You too, Aunties," Rose said. "Thank you for today."

Alexandre planted a kiss on Grace's head. "Look after your grandmother."

"I will!" Grace responded.

When the group had faded from sight, the girls sat down on the bank. Rose spied the basket she'd dropped the  day before. The evening was warm, and their feet were tired from walking. They slipped off their shoes and dangled their bare feet in the water.

"It must be so nice to have a house," Grace said with a dreamy look in her eyes. "Wherever we camp or set up for plays, that's my home. But just as I'm getting to know the best places to explore or I'm making a friend, the troupe packs everything up and moves on to the next village."

Rose thought Grace's life sounded awfully exciting. But she could hear the sadness in her new friend's voice. It reminded Rose of the voice in her head, the one that dreamed about a life other than the one in the forest. "Being in one place has its drawbacks, too," she said.

"Really?" Grace asked.

Rose sighed. "I love my aunts. I love the forest. I love the animals and the berries and the stream and the flowers and our cottage. . . ." She watched the water trickle past their feet, heading somewhere she had never been. "It can just become dull, seeing the same thing every day. It can be lonely."

Grace twirled her fingers in the stream. "It's too bad we can't switch places."

Rose laughed. "If only we knew magic and could fool everyone into thinking you're me and I'm you."

"Then *you* would get some adventure, and *I* would have one place to call my home. Just for a little while," Grace said longingly.

Rose watched a family of birds chirping on the branches overhead. She always had trouble telling two of the birds apart because they both had the same black marking on their chest, almost as though they were twins. "Perhaps we don't need magic . . . ," Rose said as an idea formed in her mind.

"What do you mean?" Grace asked.

"We both have long blond hair. We're about the same height. . . ." Rose trailed off, watching the birds. They took flight, dashing into the clouds. "I don't know what I'm saying." She shook herself. "It's foolish."

"It's not so foolish," Grace said. She stood up, excited. "From your stories, it sounds as if your aunt Merryweather is a bit . . . distracted. Might she be so distracted that she wouldn't notice if someone who looked very similar to her niece stayed in the cottage for the next few nights?"

"My aunt knows what I look like!" Rose protested.

"I want to try something. Let's switch outfits," Grace said.

Rose looked down at her simple cotton dress and black slipper shoes and then at Grace's trousers and blouse. She shrugged. The girls ducked behind some trees and exchanged clothes.

Rose tied the leather shoelaces and finished the change by wrapping herself in Grace's red cape. She saw that Grace had placed the cloak's hood over her head so it shadowed her face.

"The basket!" Rose called out. She grabbed her berry basket and placed it on Grace's wrist. Standing back, she eyed Grace—it was like looking in a mirror.

"What do you think?" Grace asked.

Rose grinned. "I think we're on to something."

Chapter 5
The Switch

The plan was simple but risky.

Grace, disguised in Rose's clothes, would head straight to Rose's bedroom upon arriving at the cottage and go to sleep. The next morning, Grace would rise before Aunt Merryweather to prepare breakfast. She'd make a mess and cover herself in flour so Aunt Merryweather wouldn't see that she wasn't Rose. She would then excuse herself to go wash up in the stream and join Rose back at the troupe's camp, where Rose would have stayed the night before. Grace promised Rose that her grandmother always went to bed early. Rose simply needed to slip into the tent, with the cape hiding her face, and go straight to Grace's bed. The next morning, when Grace returned to the camp, they would tell Madam Talia and the troupe that Rose's aunts had granted her permission to watch the rehearsals. The girls only needed to disguise themselves and switch places in the evenings, until Aunt Flora, Aunt Fauna, and Alexandre returned in three days.

After they worked out the details, Rose and Grace held hands for a moment before they went their separate ways.

"Are you sure about this?" Grace asked.

Rose was not sure. But she didn't want to waste this chance. "I think we have to try," Rose said. "Oh, and don't forget to disguise your voice so you sound more like me."

"I won't," Grace replied. She squeezed Rose's hands one last time, then slipped away into the forest.

The sun had just set by the time Rose returned to the camp. She kept the cape's hood drawn tightly around her head, nodding without looking up whenever someone shouted, "Hello, Grace!"

She found the tent that she remembered belonged to Grace's grandmother. Inside, Madam Talia was already asleep, having left a lantern on for Grace's return. A thrill ran through Rose as she climbed into Grace's bed. She'd never slept outside her cottage before. She wanted to savor every new sound, every new smell, and every new feeling, like the stiffness of Grace's straw pillow. Rose hoped Grace was enjoying her pillow of feathers, which Aunt Fauna had stuffed and stitched herself.

Rose blew out the lantern and was asleep within minutes.

"Wake up, sleepyhead!"

Rose nearly jumped out of bed when she opened her eyes, forgetting for a moment where she was. Costumes hung inches from her face. She was not in her cottage bed, and the voice calling to her did not belong to one of her aunts. It was Madam Talia!

Rose buried her head under the pillow, hoping Madam Talia hadn't seen her. She answered, her voice muffled, "Just a bit longer, Grandmother!"

The tent flap fell shut and Madam Talia left. Rose hoped Grace would arrive soon.

Thankfully, she didn't have to wait long. Rose heard the tent flap open and then Grace's voice. "It's me!" Grace darted in to Rose's side. "Hurry!" The two girls switched back to their own clothing.

"Everything went okay with Aunt Merryweather?" Rose asked. She noticed that Grace's face was still covered in flour.

Grace giggled. "Once she saw the mess I made, she tried to step in and help. If you think *my* face is covered, you should see your aunt's."

Rose laughed. "She didn't question it when you left?"

"I told her I was going to go wash in the stream," Grace said. "And she said that since the flour was already out, she would use it to make pies."

"She'll be busy all day," Rose said, helping Grace wipe off the flour. "It usually takes her about ten pies before one comes out right."

Grace peeked outside the tent. She motioned to Rose that the coast was clear.

As they strode through the campsite, Rose saw a stage had been erected between two of the center wagons. Troupe members were painting finishing touches on the backdrop: a large castle. Rose gasped at its beauty. It was as though she could step onto the stage and into another place.

"Come on," Grace called, pulling Rose toward the stage. Along the way, Grace grabbed a few hunks of bread from a table near the fire. "Good thing your aunts brought us this food!"

Rose could barely think about her breakfast, with everything there was to see. She followed Grace backstage. Everywhere Rose looked, someone was fidgeting with a costume, struggling with a prop, reciting lines, or singing notes. Grace led Rose along until they found Madam Talia stitching a costume.

"Rose!" Madam Talia beamed at her. "I'm happy you've returned."

"Rose is going to watch our rehearsals for the next few days," Grace said to her grandmother.

"Wouldn't you rather have a role *in* the play?" Madam Talia asked Rose.

Rose was taken aback. "Would that be possible?"

"Grace has a small part in the cast, and she's a member of the chorus. Have you ever heard of an understudy?"

Rose shook her head.

"An understudy," said Madam Talia, "is a member of the cast who studies someone's role in case that person needs a break or is sick and can't go on."

"You can study me," Grace suggested.

"I'd love to!" Rose said.

"Then that's settled," Madam Talia declared. "Alexandre has left me to mind the show. Let's head to the stage."

They all went to where the actors were gathered. Madam Talia clapped her hands, and the troupe immediately quieted. "Today we'll begin with the villagers' song," she announced. "Take your places, everyone!" Then she whispered in Rose's ear, "Why don't you watch a couple run-throughs and see if you can catch on?"

Rose and Madam Talia stood in front of the stage and watched the cast begin their song. The moment their mouths opened and their voices sang out together, Rose's heart soared. All her life, she'd hummed little songs with her aunts, whistled melodies with the forest birds, and sung lullabies

to the newborn animals, but she'd never heard a chorus of human voices. She was so enchanted by the music and the sound that when the song ended, she realized she hadn't been paying attention to the words!

"Again," Madam Talia called out. "Lisandra, come up a bit higher on the chorus. Nelson, try to project all the way out to the hills; we're losing your beautiful bass. And, Grace." Madam Talia smiled. "Try to project a bit *less*." Grace giggled, and the cast laughed along with her.

The chorus started their song again, and this time Rose listened to the lyrics. They sang of terrible things happening to their village: food stolen, crops dying, children scared. And it was all at the hands of an evil fairy living in the castle.

When the song ended for the second time, Madam Talia gave a few more notes, then said, "Let's take it from the top."

"May I join now?" asked Rose.

"Go ahead," Madam Talia said. "Next to Grace."

Rose scurried onto the stage and stood next to Grace. At the wave of Madam Talia's hands, the song began anew. Rose closed her eyes and let the melody guide her. She stumbled over a few of the words but remembered most of them. When the song ended and Rose opened her eyes, Madam Talia, Grace, and the rest of the cast were staring at her. "Did I do something wrong?" she asked.

"Not at all," Madam Talia said.

"You sing beautifully, Rose!" Grace said. Everyone agreed, smiling and murmuring compliments.

"Welcome to the Errant Band of Actors!" Madam Talia cried.

Chapter 6
The Legend of Maleficent

The cast rehearsed the song several more times before breaking for lunch. The troupe gathered in the center of the camp to eat. Grace ran off to find plates while Madam Talia and Rose found a log to sit on.

"Do you know the story our play is based on?" Madam Talia asked Rose.

"I've picked up bits and pieces from the song," Rose said.

"Our plays always come from legends and local tales," Madam Talia said. "This particular legend is about the evil fairy Maleficent."

Rose knew the name from the day before, when Aunt Flora had been upset by the costume. "What did she do?" she asked.

"What *hasn't* Maleficent done?" Madam Talia shook her head. "Years ago, Maleficent took up in a castle near a small village, many kingdoms away. She invited the village to her castle for a welcome reception, but no one attended, due to the frightening appearance of the place: thunderclouds and smoke, and dark creatures lurking about.

The villagers thought it was best to stay away. Offended, Maleficent exacted her revenge on the village by proclaiming herself the new ruler. Anything she wanted, the people were expected to give her, from food to weapons to horses to cloth. If they tried to resist Maleficent's demands, they'd find their crops ruined, their farm animals sick, their roofs leaking, or their meager fortunes missing.

"One day, a local maiden grew tired of watching her neighbors suffer. She went to see Maleficent in her castle and struck a deal. Maleficent demanded the maiden's beauty in exchange for leaving her village alone.

The maiden agreed instantly, for she knew that beauty was worth nothing, while her neighbors' happiness was worth everything. Maleficent cursed the maiden: she gave her scars that would never heal, she took the shine from her hair, she took the youth from her face, and she took the sweetness from her smile. But Maleficent kept her end of the bargain, and after that day, she never returned to the village. The castle, Maleficent, and her henchmen all vanished, leaving only a raven's feather behind."

Rose was horrified. "Has anyone found her? Is she still out there somewhere?"

"I'm afraid she is, child," Madam Talia said. "The stories of her terrible deeds are numerous."

"I wonder why my aunts have never told me about her," Rose said.

Just then, Grace returned, balancing three plates of food. Rose hadn't realized just how hungry she was. The story of Maleficent briefly forgotten, they set to eating and talking about the plan for the rest of the day.

After lunch, the rehearsal continued until the sunlight began to fade. Madam Talia called for an end to the practice, and the troupe started setting up for dinner.

Rose pulled Grace aside. "You'd better head back to the cottage before Aunt Merryweather gets worried."

"I was just thinking the same thing," Grace said. "Plus, I'm hungry, and I can't wait to try one of her pies!"

Rose cringed. "I'm not sure you should look forward to that. Aunt Merryweather isn't known for her cooking skills."

"Trying something new is part of the fun." Grace grinned.

The girls darted behind a tent to switch clothes, pulling their hoods up.

"On the way back to the cottage," Rose instructed, "follow the stream for the first five minutes in the forest. It will take you to a patch of blue wildflowers. Those are Aunt Merryweather's favorite, but they also make her sneeze. Carry them in front of your face when you return and she won't notice you're not me."

"Got it," Grace said.

The girls said their goodbyes, and Rose watched Grace disappear over the hill before she stepped out from behind the tent.

The campfire sparked and crackled with warm light. Rose saw a trunk of props and costume pieces near the dinner table. Some-

of the troupe members were wearing them, singing songs playfully around the fire. Rose scurried over to the trunk and selected a feathered, birdlike mask to slip over her face. She grabbed a dinner plate and sat on one of the logs near Lisandra and Nelson, who greeted her as Grace. She didn't know the songs the troupe was singing, but she hummed along joyfully and clapped her hands with the rhythm.

Madam Talia left for her tent after dinner, kissing Rose on top of her hooded head and whispering, "Good night, Grace."

The troupe sang for hours. Rose tore herself away only when she could no longer keep her eyes open. She returned the mask to the trunk, making sure her hood stayed in place, and slipped into Madam Talia's tent. Back in Grace's bed, Rose felt a twinge of guilt for all the scheming she and Grace were doing—lying to Aunt Merryweather, Madam Talia, and everyone else. But as the sounds of the campfire songs drifted into the tent, the guilt melted away. It was worth it, Rose knew in her heart. It was all worth it.

Chapter 7
A Warning

The next morning, Rose stayed under the covers again as Madam Talia left for breakfast. Soon after, Grace burst in.

As the girls switched clothing, Grace told Rose all about her time with Aunt Merryweather.

"You were right about the flowers," Grace said. "She grabbed them as soon as I walked in the door and went to find a vase.

But then she started sneezing so much, her eyes swelled up and she could barely see what was in front of her."

"Oh, no!" Rose said, but she couldn't help laughing. "And how was the pie?"

Grace adjusted her cape around her shoulders. "It was . . . different. But I'm still glad I tasted it. And I love your cottage. Everything has its place. Things aren't piled into satchels and trunks, ready to be moved at a moment's notice. And the forest . . ." She swooned.

Rose felt a tug in her heart at hearing Grace talk about her home so affectionately.

"How did you get away this morning?" Rose asked.

"It was easy," Grace said. "Your aunt was busy mending skirts when I came downstairs, muttering about how much she had to do before Flora and Fauna return tomorrow. She'd managed to sew two of the skirts completely closed!"

Rose chuckled. "She's done that before. She always figures it out in the end."

"Anyhow, she was distracted enough that I could slip away." Grace smoothed her cape. "Shall we?"

The day was filled with more songs,

a dance, and several other scenes from the play. Grace had only a couple of speaking lines, but Madam Talia let Rose stand in and practice twice.

At lunchtime, Rose noticed Madam Talia speaking to a tall woman with dark hair.

"That's Antoinette," Grace said. "She's playing Maleficent."

Antoinette was laughing with Madam Talia, her face gentle and kind. It was hard to imagine this lovely woman playing such a sinister character. But then Madam Talia lifted the pointed headdress and helped Antoinette secure it on her head. Suddenly, a look of cool malevolence took over the

woman's face. It was as though she'd become a different person! Rose shuddered.

"She's so talented, isn't she?" Grace asked. "They're getting her costume ready for the dress rehearsal tomorrow."

Talent. That's what it must be, Rose thought as she watched Antoinette remove the headdress. The woman's pleasant nature returned. Rose knew it was an act, the way she had transformed with just a piece of her costume on her head. But the voice of her aunt echoed in her mind. *Evil can be disguised.* If Rose could be momentarily fooled by *fake* evil, how would she ever know how to recognize the real thing?

"Can we eat now?" Grace asked. "I'm starving!"

"Of course," Rose said. But as she ate her lunch, she wished she were eating one of her aunt Merryweather's pies.

The afternoon rehearsal went by even faster than the morning's had. Soon it was time for Grace and Rose to switch clothes again.

"I wish you could come to the dress rehearsal tomorrow evening," Grace said.

"Me too." Rose handed Grace her cloak. The girls were huddled behind a tent, out of view of the rest of the troupe. "But I'll stick to the regular morning rehearsal. Aunt

Flora and Aunt Fauna will probably be back by midday."

"It's too bad they haven't been able to see what you've been learning here," Grace said. "I overheard my grandmother talking about you. She said she's never seen such natural talent."

Rose felt her cheeks burning. "That's awfully nice of her."

Grace started to walk toward the forest, when Rose called out in a loud whisper, "We haven't discussed how you'll disguise yourself at the cottage tonight!"

"Don't worry," Grace said, turning around. "I'll think of something!"

Rose waved goodbye to her friend. She would skip the singing and dinner. It was her last night to explore, and she was curious about what was in the wagons. In the first wagon on the left, she found maps tacked to the canvas walls. Rose had to cover her mouth to keep from squealing. Right in front of her were sketches of kingdoms, lands—the whole country! She traced her fingers along the roads, imagining what the squiggly lines looked like in real life.

Voices approached, causing Rose to duck behind an empty trunk. They stopped right outside the front of the wagon. She recognized one voice as Madam Talia's. The other belonged to a man.

". . . concerned," the man was saying. "The bandits could still be in the area."

"But why would they stick around?" Madam Talia asked.

"They didn't get everything the first time," the man said.

"I'd rather not worry anyone unnecessarily," Madam Talia said. "Alexandre and the others will be back tomorrow, and then we'll be on our way."

"I understand,

Talia. But the campsite we discovered looked suspicious."

"We'll keep watch tonight, then," Madam Talia said.

Rose heard their footsteps walking away. She breathed a sigh of relief at not being discovered, and then another thought struck her. *Bandits. Still in the area?*

Rose wasted no time in hurrying back to Madam Talia's tent and climbing into bed. She didn't bother with dinner. Her stomach was too tied up in knots to think of food.

She pulled the covers over her head and tried to go to sleep. But thoughts of bandits, Grace, and her aunts filled her mind.

Chapter 8
Another Rescue

After a restless night, Rose woke, surprised that Grace wasn't already there. But she quickly came up with a plan. If Grace didn't show up by the time breakfast was over, she would gather the actors to check on her.

As Rose waited, her nerves bundled tighter and tighter. Finally, she gave up and crept toward the opening of the tent. The troupe was finishing breakfast. There was no sign of Grace.

Rose took a deep breath and walked across the campsite toward Madam Talia.

"Rose!" Madam Talia greeted her. "Could you wake Grace? Wait, why are you wearing *her* clothes?"

Rose gulped. "Madam Talia . . . I have a confession."

The story of Rose and Grace's switch came tumbling out. Rose summarized as quickly as she could to get to the most important part: "What if Grace ran into the bandits? Oh, Madam Talia, I'm so worried. I'm so sorry!"

The old woman gripped Rose's shoulders and looked her in the eyes. "Rose, thank you for telling me the truth. It was the right thing to do." Madam Talia called over to the stage: "Nelson, Lisandra, Kenneth—could you join us?"

The three actors hurried over. "We have reason to worry that Grace may have run into trouble in the forest," Madam Talia explained. "Rose, we'll need you to lead us on the route you take to your cottage."

Rose led the small search party over the hill and toward the stream that marked the edge of the forest. She wished that crossing the stream would take her back to a time when everyone she knew and cared about was safe.

"Grace!" Madam Talia shouted when they'd reached the line of trees.

"Grace!" the others cried out, moving into the forest.

"Grace!" Rose called. In the distance, she saw the large hollowed-out tree she often used when she played hide-and-seek with the rabbits. But now she saw there were branches piled up near the opening.

Rose raced to the tree trunk. "Over here!" She'd told Grace all about it on the day they'd met. She cleared the branches aside and saw a bit of blond hair.

"Grace!" Rose cried, reaching into the opening. She felt Grace's hand grasp her own, holding tight. Rose helped her friend, covered in dirt, crawl out.

Madam Talia rushed over.

"I'm okay," Grace said. "Just a little dirty."

"What happened?" Rose asked.

Grace looked at her grandmother, then at Rose.

"I told her everything," Rose said.

Grace bit her lip. "On my way back to the campsite this morning, I spotted some strangers by the stream getting water. I hid and listened to what they were saying. They

were talking about heading to the road and robbing the wagons again tonight. I wanted to run and warn everyone, but I stepped on a branch and they turned around and saw me! I got away and was able to hide in here. I was afraid to come out until I heard you. But it hasn't been that long; we can still find them!"

Madam Talia turned to Nelson, Lisandra, and Kenneth. "Lisandra, go back to camp and warn the others. Nelson and Kenneth, go to the road and see if you can intercept these scoundrels."

Nelson, Lisandra, and Kenneth took off, out of the forest.

Madam Talia scowled at Rose and Grace.

"I don't need to tell you what a foolish and dangerous scheme this was. You're both smart girls who ought to know better. And that's the most troubling part. If you *knew* better, why didn't you *do* better?"

Grace started to speak, but her grandmother interrupted: "I'm in charge of looking after you, Grace. Imagine if something had happened to you? And, Rose—did you even have permission to come and participate in our rehearsals?"

Rose shook her head, ashamed. "I just wanted to experience some of the outside world, to be around other people," she said.

"And I just wanted to know what a real home felt like," said Grace.

"I'm sorry," they said in unison.

"And I'm sorry that you felt you had to trick me and Rose's aunts in order to get what you wanted," said Madam Talia as she brushed some of the remaining dirt from Grace's cloak. "Now please show me the way to the cottage. I have a feeling your aunt Merryweather will want to hear this story, too."

Chapter 9
Flora and Fauna Return

$\mathcal{A}$unt Merryweather was on her way out of the cottage when Rose, Grace, and Madam Talia approached. Her cheeks went from flushed with surprise to deep red with anger when Rose explained what she and Grace had been up to for the past few days. It was an awful feeling to see her aunt so upset and betrayed.

"I was just heading out to find the

campsite and welcome Flora and Fauna upon their return." Aunt Merryweather shook her head. "I was going to ask if you wanted to come along, Rose. As a special treat."

Rose bowed her head. "I'm so sorry. I'll go straight to my room."

"Oh, no," Aunt Merryweather said. "I'm keeping my eye on you. You're coming with me."

"It would be nice to have an escort back to camp," Madam Talia said. "I was so distracted with worry for Grace, I wasn't paying much attention to the route here."

"Of course," Aunt Merryweather said. "Though it seems your granddaughter knows the way." She looked pointedly at Grace.

Grace gave an embarrassed smile.

"That was really you for the last few days?" Aunt Merryweather asked Grace.

"I enjoyed being your temporary niece," Grace said shyly.

Aunt Merryweather sighed as she began walking toward the edge of the forest, the rest of the group following. "At least you didn't complain about my cooking," she said. "I suppose that should have been a clue that something was different."

When they returned to the campsite, Rose was grateful to see that no bandits had shown up—yet.

"No sign of Nelson or Kenneth," Lisandra said. "We—"

Lisandra was interrupted by shouts of excitement. Marching down the road were Nelson and Kenneth, followed by Aunt Flora, Aunt Fauna, Alexandre, and the others who'd journeyed with them to the village. Behind them were three bandits, each one tied up with rope.

Madam Talia and Aunt Merryweather ran to greet the new arrivals. Kenneth, Nelson, and the other men led the bound bandits away.

"You wouldn't believe it," Alexandre

boasted, loud enough for Rose to hear. "We were on our way back with the wagon wheels, when we saw Nelson and Kenneth. Then suddenly, those bandits jumped out at them! Well, before I had a chance to react, these brave ladies"—he motioned to Aunt Flora and Aunt Fauna—"secured the bandits with ropes!"

Rose and Grace looked at each other in awe. "Your aunts caught the bandits? They're incredible!" Grace said.

"They sure are," Rose agreed.

"What will you do with the bandits now?" Aunt Fauna asked Alexandre.

"We'll take them along with us to the

next village, where we can turn them in to the proper authorities," Alexandre said.

"We won't let them out of our sight," Madam Talia added.

"Ahem." Aunt Merryweather cleared her throat. "Speaking of letting things out of our sight . . ." She pointed to Rose and Grace.

"Rose! What are you doing here?" Aunt Flora asked.

Rose swallowed. "I have a story of my own to tell."

Rose and Grace told Aunt Flora, Aunt Fauna, and Alexandre what they'd been up to for the past three days. When they finished, Rose's aunts were so stunned, she worried they'd forgotten how to speak.

Alexandre broke the silence. "I think we'll leave you for a moment to have a family discussion." He eyed Grace. "While we have one of our own." He led Grace away, and Madam Talia followed.

"I don't understand, Rose," Aunt Flora said. "You know you aren't supposed to leave the forest, let alone permit a stranger to enter our cottage."

"Grace isn't a stranger," Rose said.

"She isn't now, dear," Aunt Fauna said. "But you barely knew her, or Madame Talia, when you started this."

"You made me look pretty foolish," Aunt Merryweather said with a huff.

"I'm truly sorry," Rose said. "Please understand that none of this was to hurt you. I just saw a chance to live a dream, and I took it."

"We want you to live your dreams, dear Rose," Aunt Fauna said. "But you also need

to follow the rules we set, or there could be disastrous consequences. Much worse than what happened today."

"I realize there is darkness in the world," Rose said. "I realize there are people out there who do bad things. I understand that better now. But I also don't want to hide forever."

"Of course not," Aunt Merryweather said sympathetically.

"For the next two weeks, however, you will be confined to the cottage. No berry picking, no stream wading, and no animal visiting. Is that quite clear?" Aunt Flora asked Rose.

"Very clear," Rose said.

"You'd better go change and say your goodbyes, then," Aunt Fauna told her.

Near Madam Talia's tent, Grace was finishing up her own conversation with her father and grandmother.

Madam Talia turned to Rose's aunts. "Could I speak with you for a moment while they change?"

Grace and Rose ducked into the tent. "What do you think that's about?" Grace asked Rose as they began their final clothes swap.

"Maybe they want to trade notes on punishments?" Rose removed Grace's cape.

"Are you in terrible trouble?" Grace asked.

"I have to stay in the cottage for two weeks," Rose said. "What about you?"

"Meal cooking *and* cleanup duty through our next ten performances," Grace groaned.

"Worth it?" Rose asked. The girls were back in their own clothes. It felt right.

"Worth it," Grace said with a grin.

They emerged from the tent and found Madam Talia smiling next to Rose's aunts.

"Rose," Aunt Flora began, "we've been speaking to Madame Talia, who has nothing but praise for your behavior and talent these last few days. Considering you ultimately did the right thing in speaking up and telling the truth, we're going to make an exception—"

"—and let you stay for the dress rehearsal!" Aunt Merryweather cheered.

Rose clapped her hands to her face in surprise. "Oh, my! Thank you!" She raced to her aunts and gathered them in a hug. She felt like the luckiest girl in the world.

Chapter 10
The Show Goes On

That evening, the troupe's campsite was magical to behold. The blaze of the fire was joined by the glow of dozens of lanterns hanging from the tents, wagons, and stage. The scene was buzzing with excitement as colorful costumed figures dashed about.

Rose settled her aunts in the audience before heading backstage to find Grace and her grandmother.

"Grace!" Rose exclaimed. "You aren't in your costume. The dress rehearsal is about to start!"

Grace was in her usual red cape. She let out a pitiful cough. "I've just come down with something. I can't go on." She flung her hand to her forehead dramatically.

"This is what we have understudies for." Madam Talia winked, pointing to Grace's costume. She helped Rose into the simple frock.

"Are you sure?" Rose asked Grace.

"I'm sure!" Grace answered cheerily, not sounding sick at all. "I'll go watch with your aunts." She ran off.

Rose and Madam Talia walked to the stage wings. "I ought to go out and make sure it's all right with my aunts that I perform," Rose said.

"I asked for their blessing earlier, when we spoke," Madam Talia said. "I also asked that it be a surprise."

Rose peeked around the curtain at the audience. Her aunts and Grace waved at her. She waved back and happily returned to Madam Talia's side.

"You acted bravely under pressure today, Rose," Madam Talia said. "You told the truth when the truth wasn't easy to tell."

Rose shrugged. "Grace could have been in trouble."

"Not everyone has such pure instincts. The world can be a cruel place," Madam Talia said. "But that is why it's important to recognize good people who do good things. For I believe there are many more good people than bad people."

"I hope my aunts believe that, too," Rose said with a sigh.

"Your aunts are looking out for you."

Madam Talia reached into her robes and withdrew a raven feather, long and black. Rose wondered if it was a prop from the play. "I understand what it feels like to want to protect those you care about. I've kept this for many years as a reminder."

Rose gasped. It wasn't just a prop. The story of the play, about the maiden who'd stood up to Maleficent, and Madam Talia's scars, all took on new meaning. "*You* were the maiden?" Rose asked. "*You're* the one who was cursed by Maleficent?"

Madam Talia put a finger to her lips. "Don't say it too loudly. I'm waiting until Grace is older to tell her."

Rose felt honored that Madam Talia was entrusting her with such a secret. "But why are you telling me?"

"When I was young, I was often underestimated because of my beauty. People thought I was only capable of polite conversation. They laughed when I spoke of my dreams to work on the stage and create stories. But I knew that beauty was far from my greatest gift. That is why I did not hesitate to give it to Maleficent. I knew I still had the ability to love, to tell stories, to sing, and to laugh. Evil tries to take away your power—but if you're strong, you let it show you your power instead. You let it show you what's most important. You don't have to let it win."

"I certainly don't want to encounter evil," Rose said. "But I'd like to be strong. I'd like to learn my own power."

"You're on your way," Madam Talia said. "Keep dreaming, Rose. I have a feeling your story will be a good one."

It was a night Rose would not soon forget. She'd been a part of something: of a cast, of songs, of a story. And it felt like a wonderful dream come true.

After the dress rehearsal ended, everyone at the campsite took a moment to speak with

Rose and her aunts. They thanked them for helping out with the wagons, for finding Grace, and most of all, for capturing the bandits.

When it came time to say goodbye to Madam Talia, Rose wrapped her in a hug and whispered in her ear, "Thank you for everything. I'll keep your secret safe, I promise."

"Take care of yourself, Rose," Madam Talia replied.

Rose turned to Grace. "I'm so glad you came to my forest looking for water."

"And I'm so glad—well, I'm not glad the bunny got hurt, but I'm glad it gave me the chance to meet you," Grace said. The girls squeezed each other tight.

My first friend, Rose thought with a smile.

As she headed up the hill with her aunts,

Rose glanced back more than once to see the troupe packing up their wagons and preparing for another journey. Though she wondered what else was out in the world, she felt comfort in knowing she was heading back to a home that didn't change, that was always there.

"You know, Flora," Aunt Fauna said as they neared the edge of the forest, "I hear there are delicious berries near the

waterfall—plump, wild red ones. Have you ever tasted them?"

"I have!" Aunt Flora said. "They were delicious."

"It's lovely over by the waterfall," Aunt Merryweather said. "A gorgeous view."

"Rose, you ought to pick some for us," Aunt Fauna said. "After two weeks have passed, of course."

Rose eyed her aunts. Was this a test? "Aunt Fauna, you know the waterfall is beyond the fallen tree. I've never even seen it because you haven't let me go that far!"

"Perhaps it's time to expand the borders a bit," Aunt Merryweather said.

"Do you mean it?" Rose squealed.

Aunt Flora nodded. "How about the waterfall to the west, the caves to the south, the strawberry bushes to the north—"

"And the road to the east?" Rose interrupted.

"And the stream to the east," Aunt Flora corrected her. "One step at a time, Rose."

"Yes, Aunt Flora. Thank you all for trusting me—you won't be sorry!"

One step at a time, thought Rose.

And someday she would step into the rest of the world beyond her borders and discover her true identity—Princess Aurora!